DORA SAVES THE ENCHANTED FOREST

adapted by Sheila Sweeny Higginson
based on the screenplay "Dora Saves King Unicornio"
written by Valerie Walsh Valdes
illustrated by Victoria Miller

SIMON AND SCHUSTER/NICKELODEON

Simon and Schuster
First published in Great Britain in 2011 by Simon & Schuster UK Ltd
1st Floor, 222 Gray's Inn Road, London WC1X 8HB
A CBS Company

Originally published in the USA in 2011 by Simon Spotlight,
an imprint of Simon & Schuster Children's Division, New York.

A CIP catalogue record for this book is available from the British Library

ISBN 978-0-85707-260-3
Printed in Great Britain
10 9 8 7 6 5 4 3 2 1

Visit our websites:
www.simonandschuster.co.uk
www.nickjr.co.uk

Once upon a time, there was a magical land called the Enchanted Forest. King Unicornio, a kind and fair leader, ruled over the forest. All of the creatures there were free to do what they wanted to do. Honeybees could sing. Puppy dogs could try to fly and Oak trees could play hide-and-seek.

One sad day, everything changed. King Unicornio had to leave the Enchanted Forest so he gave his crown to Owl and asked him to watch over the kingdom. But Owl was not kind and fair like Unicornio. He made new rules. He said that bees could not sing and dogs could not try to fly.

When Unicornio returned, Owl did not want to give the crown back. The sneaky bird led Unicornio into a trap! Owl put a crack in the dam, and King Unicornio had to use his magic horn to plug the crack. If Unicornio didn't stay where he was, the Enchanted Forest would flood. So all of the creatures in the forest had to keep following Owl's unfair rules!

The creatures of the Enchanted Forest were not happy with Owl's rules. They wanted Unicornio to be their king, and they knew there was only one person who could help them. Dora!

Can you see the way to get to the Enchanted Forest? Use your finger to show Dora the way to go.

Rabbit set out from the forest to look for her. He hopped through the Fairy Tunnel and past the Elf Garden. He hopped across the Cornfield and found Dora and Boots playing outside Dora's house.

"¡Dora, Boots, *vengan rápido!*" Rabbit called to his friends. "We've got to rescue Unicornio so he can be king again! Can you help to save the Enchanted Forest?"

"We've got to find the quickest way to the Enchanted Forest," Dora answered. "Map can help us!"

Dora and Boots headed down the path to get to the Cornfield. There they saw a scarecrow perched on his pole.

"*iHola,* Scarecrow*!*" Dora called. "Can we go through the Cornfield, *por favor*?"

Before the Scarecrow could answer, Owl flew by.

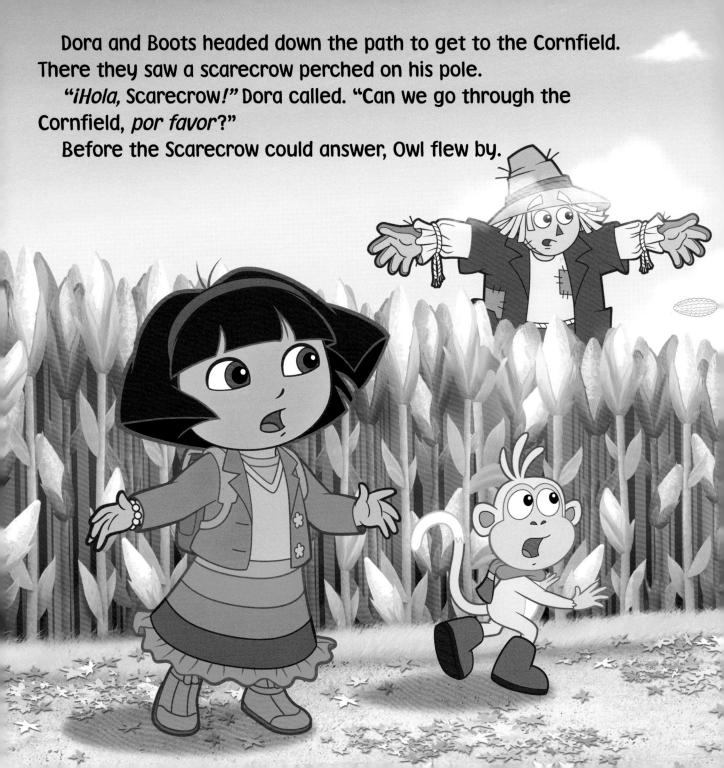

Owl didn't want Dora to help Unicornio. He wanted to be king forever! He told the mini-owls to pile up lots and lots of corn so Dora and Boots could not get to the Enchanted Forest.

Scarecrow was happy to help Dora and Boots find a way to clear the path.

"Owl made a new rule," Scarecrow told them. "He said that scarecrows and crows can't go into the Enchanted Forest anymore."

"That's not fair!" Dora and Boots cried.

"I have an idea," said Dora.

"If we invite the crows down, instead of chasing them away, they could clean up the path," Dora said to Scarecrow.

"Okay, I'll give it a try," Scarecrow replied. He called out *"¡Bienvenidos, amigos!"* to the crows. That's how you say "Welcome, friends!" in Spanish.

Dora's plan worked like a charm. The crows picked up all of the corn. They cleared the path so Dora and Boots could head to their next stop – the Elf Garden!

"*¡Vámonos,* Boots*!*" Dora called. "Let's go!"

Dora and Boots raced down the path to the Elf Garden. Before they could get across the bridge that led to the garden, Owl flew by. He didn't want Dora to help Unicornio. He wanted to be king forever! He told the mini-owls to take the screws out of the bridge so Dora and Boots could not get to the Enchanted Forest.

The elves can fix the bridge if they work together. Will you work with them? Point to the pieces and show where they belong.

The elves were happy to help Dora and Boots find a way to fix the bridge.

"Owl made a new rule," the elves told them. "He said that elves can't go into the Enchanted Forest anymore."

"That's not fair!" Dora and Boots cried as they raced to the Fairy Tunnel.

Up ahead, the firefly fairies were shimmering around a patch of sunflowers. Dora knew the fairies could use their light to show them the way through the dark tunnel.

Before they could get to the tunnel, Owl flew by. He didn't want Dora to help Unicornio. So he told the mini-owls to blow out the fairies' lights. Dora and Boots could not get to the Enchanted Forest.

The little fairy still has her light. Will you make it grow? Rub your hands together to make more light!

The fairies were happy to help Dora and Boots find a way through the tunnel.

"Owl made a new rule," the fairies told them. "He said that fairies can't go into the Enchanted Forest anymore."

"That's not fair!" Dora and Boots cried as they headed to the Enchanted Forest.

Dora and Boots were ready to rescue King Unicornio. They had made it across the Cornfield, past the Elf Garden, and through the Fairy Tunnel. There was just one thing left for them to do. They had to open the magic door that led to the Enchanted Forest.

Can you say the magic words to open the door? *¡Puerta mágica!* That means "magic door." Say *"¡Puerta mágica!"*

Dora and Boots had made it to the Enchanted Forest. They were sad to see how much it had changed. There were no scarecrows or elves in the forest. There were no fairies in the forest. Owl had even told the squirrels that they weren't allowed in the Enchanted Forest anymore!

Rabbit came hopping over to Dora and Boots.

"I'll take you to Unicornio," he whispered to them. "He's protecting the forest with his horn."

"We've got to help him!" Dora agreed as she followed Rabbit.

Before they could get to the dam, Owl flew by. He didn't want Dora to help Unicornio. He wanted to be king forever! He told the mini-owls to make more leaks so Dora and Boots had to stay to plug the dam too!

Dora looked over at the kind and fair Unicornio. He was so brave and loyal. He was not just a great leader, he was a good friend, too.

"Good friends, that's it!" Dora cried. "We made lots of friends today. Maybe they can help us one more time."

Dora and Boots thought about the friends they met on their way to the Enchanted Forest. The elves were really good at fixing things, so Dora sent Rabbit to find them.

"Tell the elves to bring their tools!" she called to Rabbit as he hopped away. *"¡Rapido!"*

Quick as a flash, the elves came with their tools. They were eager to help fix the dam so that Unicornio could return to the Enchanted Forest.

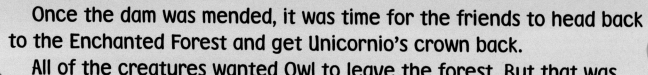

Once the dam was mended, it was time for the friends to head back to the Enchanted Forest and get Unicornio's crown back.

All of the creatures wanted Owl to leave the forest. But that was not fair either. The Enchanted Forest was for everyone!

"Owl, you are very smart, but you must learn to get along with others and treat everyone fairly," Unicornio told him. "I want you to do a service for everyone in the forest."

Owl was told to invite everyone to the biggest party the Enchanted Forest has ever seen. Then Owl returned the crown to King Unicornio. All of the creatures celebrated King Unicornio's return to the throne. They danced and sang as fireworks flashed in the sky.

¡Viva el rey Unicornio*!* Long live King Unicornio!